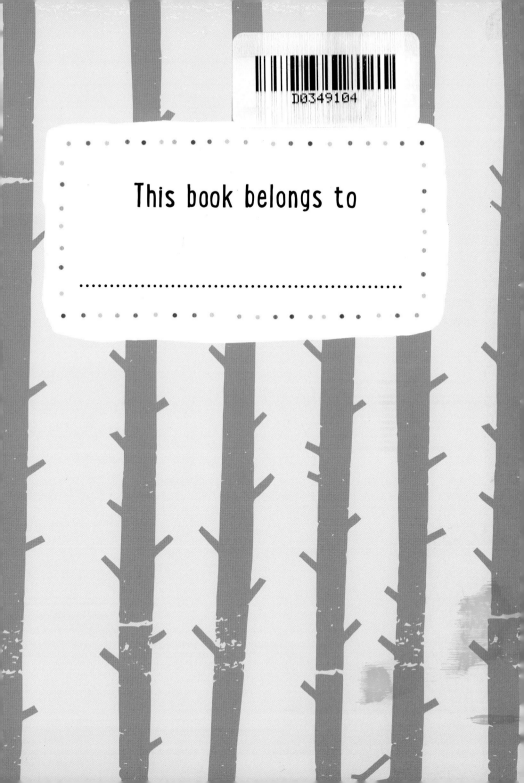

This book belongs to

....

This edition published by Parragon Books Ltd in 2017

Parragon Books Ltd
Chartist House
15–17 Trim Street
Bath BA1 1HA, UK
www.parragon.com

Illustrated by: Mei Matsuoka
Reading consultant: Geraldine Taylor

ISBN 978-1-4748-9517-0

Printed in China

My First Storytime
The Three Little Pigs

PaRragon

Bath · New York · Cologne · Melbourne · Delhi
Hong Kong · Shenzhen · Singapore

Five steps for enjoyable reading

Traditional stories and fairy tales are a great way to begin reading practice. The stories and characters are familiar and lively. Follow the steps below to help your child become a confident and independent reader:

The three little pigs waved goodbye to their mum. They were going to explore the big, wide world.
"Bye bye," called Mum. "And remember, keep away from the Big Bad Wolf!"

Step 1
Read the story aloud to your child. Run your finger under the words as you read.

Step 2
Look at the pictures and talk about what is happening.

8

Step 3
Read the simple text on the right-hand page together. When reading, some words come up again and again, such as **the, to, and**. Your child will quickly get to recognize these high-frequency words by sight.

The three little pigs set off.

Step 4
When your child is ready, encourage them to read the simple lines on their own.

Step 5
Help your child to complete the puzzles at the back of the book.

The three little pigs waved goodbye to their mum. They were going to explore the big, wide world.

"Bye bye," called Mum. "And remember, keep away from the Big Bad Wolf!"

The three little pigs set off.

Soon, the first little pig met a man pulling a cart full of straw.

"Please can I buy your straw to build my house?" asked the first little pig. The man was happy to sell his straw. He was tired of pulling his heavy cart!

The first little pig made a house
of straw.

But that night, the Big Bad Wolf came to call.

"Little pig, let me in," he called.

"No fear!" said the first little pig. So the wolf huffed and puffed and blew the house down.

The first little pig ran away.

The second little pig met
a man chopping trees in
the woods.

"Please can I buy some
sticks to build my house?"
asked the second little pig.
The man was happy to sell
his sticks. He had been
chopping them all day!

The second little pig made his
house in no time.

But can you guess who came to call? The Big Bad Wolf.

"Little pig, let me in," he called.

"No fear!" said the second little pig. So the wolf huffed and puffed, and puffed again, and blew the house down.

The second little pig ran away as fast as he could.

The third little pig found
some bricks.

"I'm going to build my house
with bricks," said the third
little pig to himself.

He carried the bricks to the
top of a little hill. He laid the
bricks. He hammered and
sawed. He put on the roof
and the windows and doors.
His brick house took a long
time to build.

The third little pig had
a good, strong house.

No sooner had the third little pig finished his house, than he saw the other two little pigs. They were running as fast as they could because the Big Bad Wolf was chasing after them!

"Come and hide in here," he called.

The two little pigs came rushing inside and the third little pig slammed the door shut.

"Go away, you Big Bad Wolf," they shouted. But the Big Bad Wolf wouldn't go away.

"Let me in," he called.

"You can't come in," said the three little pigs.

So the Big Bad Wolf huffed and puffed. Nothing happened. He huffed and puffed again. Still nothing happened. The Big Bad Wolf blew so hard he made himself dizzy. The three little pigs were safe inside the brick house.

The brick house was too strong for
the Big Bad Wolf to blow down.

"I'm coming to get you," growled the wolf. He started to climb down the chimney.

The three little pigs were cooking a big pot of hot soup on the fire. The wolf came down and landed, plop, in the soup!

"Yow!" he shouted and ran out of the house as fast as he could!

And the three little pigs never
saw the Big Bad Wolf again.

Puzzle time!

Which two words rhyme?

his bad big run pig

Which word does not match the picture?

house

straw

chimney

Which word matches the picture?

brick

stick

click

You can't come in.

You can come in.

Which sentence is right?

third little pig

wolf

first little pig

Who falls in the pot?